Lulu the Shy Piglet

Written by So-yun Jeong
Illustrated by Laura Orsolini
Edited by Joy Cowley

big & SMALL

Lulu the piglet was kind.

Lulu the piglet was a good singer.

But Lulu was so shy

that her voice was a tiny squeak.

Lulu's cheeks turned red.
She ran into the house
and sat all by herself.
Poor Lulu!

Lulu's face is on fire!

Lulu is hiding!

5

Lulu's favourite place
was an old empty barn.
When Lulu was there,
she felt happy and calm.
She could sing a happy song
because no one was listening.

Well, almost no one.

A little mouse said, "Wow!
You sing like a star!
You should be on a stage!"

Lulu's heart jumped
and her face turned red.

The mouse said to her,
"Your cheeks are on fire,
but that is okay.
Just keep on singing."

But it wasn't okay.
Lulu ran away.

The next day,
Lulu was walking along
with her head down,
when someone ran up to her.

"Hi, again!"
It was that mouse.

Lulu was still embarrassed
so she pretended not to hear.

The mouse shouted at her,
"Let's be friends!"

The mouse put black sunglasses
on Lulu the piglet.
"This is a friendship gift," he said.
"Do you feel less shy?
Do you feel more brave?
That's because these glasses
get rid of shyness."

"Oh! Really?" said Lulu.

Lulu walked around the farm.
She didn't hang her head.
She looked at the other animals
and they looked at her.
She even smiled at them.
She felt very confident
with her special glasses.

Lulu's voice got louder
and her face was not as red.

"You did it! You are so brave!"
said the mouse.

Lulu was so pleased
that she sang for her friend.

The mouse clapped and clapped.
"Tomorrow you can sing
for all the farm animals."

Lulu smiled and nodded.

Lulu was very pleased
that she was going to sing.
But she tripped over Miss Sheep
and her black sunglasses flew off.

They landed on the ground
just as Mr Ox stepped backwards.

"What's the matter, Lulu?"
asked the mouse.

Lulu sobbed, "I can't sing today.
My glasses are broken."

The mouse said gently,
"Lulu, look at your reflection.
Nothing has changed.
The voice that got louder is yours.
The beautiful singing is yours.
It's not the sunglasses, Lulu.
It is you!
You don't need the glasses."

That evening,
the animals went to the barn.
They asked each other,
"Who is this great star
that is going to sing?"

Then in walked Lulu.

The animals cried out,
"It is Fire Cheeks Lulu!"

23

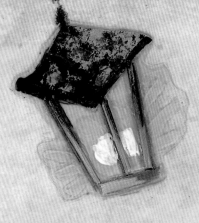

Lulu said in a shaky voice,
"I'm very nervous
but I will do my best."

The animals cheered
and that made her feel better.
She began to sing.

Her voice was beautiful.
Everyone wanted her to sing
over and over again.

24

She's a star!

Beautiful!

Dear Lulu,

Today you were fantastic!
You are the star of our farm.
We think you are amazing
because you sing well.
You are even more amazing
because you overcame your shyness
to sing for all the animals.
You don't need dark sunglasses any more.
If you get nervous, be nervous.
If you feel shy, be shy.
Don't run away and hide.
Be what you are.
When you get courage,
you shine like the treasure
that you really are.

Your friend,
Mouse

big&SMALL

Original Korean text by So-yun Jeong
Illustrations by Laura Orsolini
Original Korean edition © Eenbook 2011

This English edition published by Big & Small in 2015
by arrangement with Eenbook
English text edited by Joy Cowley
Additional editing by Mary Lindeen
Artwork for this edition produced
in cooperation with Norwood House Press, USA
English edition © Big & Small 2015

ISBN: 978-1-925233-99-5

Printed in Korea